For Oscar

First published 1994 by
Walker Books Ltd
87 Vauxhall Walk
London SE11 5HJ

This edition published 1998

2 4 6 8 10 9 7 5 3 1

© 1994 Catherine and Laurence Anholt

This book has been typeset in Bembo.

Printed in Hong Kong

British Library Cataloguing in Publication Data
A catalogue record for this book is
available from the British Library.

ISBN 0-7445-6190-6 (Hbk)
ISBN 0-7445-6069-1 (Pbk)

WHAT MAKES ME HAPPY?

Catherine and Laurence Anholt

WALKER BOOKS

AND SUBSIDIARIES

LONDON • BOSTON • SYDNEY

What makes me laugh?

tickly toes

a big red nose

being rude

silly food

acting crazy

my friend Maisie

What makes me cry?

wasps that sting

a fall from a swing

wobbly wheels

head over heels

What makes me bored?

Grown-ups…

moaning   groaning   eating   meeting   walking   talking

feeding   reading   sitting   knitting   stopping   shopping

What makes me pleased?

Look how much I've grown!

I can do it on my own!

What makes us jealous?

Her!

What makes me scared?

shrieks

creaks

jaws

claws

bangs

gangs

caves

waves

What makes me sad?

Rain, rain, every day.

No one wants to let me play.

Someone special's far away.

What makes us excited?

A roller-coaster ride

Here comes the bride!

The monster's on his way!

A party day

What makes me shy?

My first day

What makes me cross?

Days when buttons won't go straight
and I want to stay up late
and I hate what's on my plate…
Why won't anybody wait?

What makes us all happy?

making a castle

opening a parcel

singing a song   skipping along

windy weather   finding a feather and...

Being together.